For my little Stellan possum who says, "Don't be shy!"—BJ

To Jerome, for giving me the chance to blossom—JM

Published by
Magination Press ®
An Educational Publishing Foundation Book
American Psychological Association
750 First Street NE
Washington, DC 20002

Magination Press is a registered trademark of the American Psychological Association.

For more information about our books, including a complete catalog, please write to us, call 1-800-374-2721, or visit our website at www.apa.org/pubs/magination.

Book design by Susan K. White
Printed by Worzalla, Stevens Point, WI

Library of Congress Cataloging-in-Publication Data

Library of Congress Cataloging-in-Publication Data
Names: Jones, Birdy, author. | McDonnell, Janet, 1962- illustrator.
Title: Blossom plays possum : (because she's shy) / by Birdy Jones ; illustrated by Janet McDonnell.
Description: Washington, DC : Magination Press, American Psychological Association, [2017] |
Summary: Blossom, a shy possum, is nervous about trying new things but, with advice from a teacher and some practice, she finds the courage to try new things.
Identifiers: LCCN 2016049686| ISBN 9781433827358 (hardback) | ISBN 1433827352 (hardback)
Subjects: | CYAC: Anxiety—Fiction. | Bashfulness—Fiction. | Schools—Fiction. | Opossums—Fiction.
Classification: LCC PZ7.1.J655 Blo 2017 | DDC [E]—dc23 LC record available at https://lccn.loc.gov/2016049686

Manufactured in the United States of America
10 9 8 7 6 5 4 3 2 1

Ask me my name?

Want me to play?

Call on me in class?

I say nothing and hope no one will see me.

I call that playing possum.
It's my way of being shy.

I also get stage fright,

feel nervous when I have to sit next to someone I don't know,

and don't look people in the eye.

But those aren't the only things I do.

I make my own Glitter Glam headbands,

jam on my flute,

and recite poetry by heart.

But no one knows that because
I play possum before they find out.

At lunch I eat a peanut butter and granola sandwich.

Rufus says, "YUCK! Who eats that for lunch?"

I want to tell him it's the best sandwich in the world
but I freeze up.

He calls me a weirdo and sits with his friends.

The only thing sitting with me is my sandwich.

On the playground I hear some girls singing my favorite songs.

Gladys asks if I'd like to sing with them.

Instead I hang upside down on the monkey bars
like a possum would.

I'm scared they'll laugh if they hear my squeaky voice.

They have fun singing without me.

What did he mean, "see it another way"?

Then in art, I'm picked to pose for the whole class.

I'm so embarrassed I play possum
by lying on the floor and covering my eyes.

I wait for everyone to start laughing at me…but instead Otis says, "Your pose is so natural. This is my best drawing ever!"

The class asks if I will do it again and I think about it.

Maybe trying new things isn't as bad as I thought.

The next day Mr. Brass asks,
"Blossom, are you ready to play today?"

I shake my head. "Okay. Maybe tomorrow," he smiles.

But what if I make a mistake? It's easier playing possum.

Then I remember what he told me.
"Try to see it another way."

Ramona played a few wrong notes last week,
but I still liked listening to her.

Maybe they will like my playing,
even if I make some mistakes.

In science, Mrs. Fuzz asks, "What baby animal is carried in a pouch, likes nighttime, and can play dead?" She has a glittery sticker for the kid who gets it right.

I close my eyes and raise my paw, even though I have butterflies in my tummy.

Mrs. Fuzz calls on me. "Possums!" I squeak.

This sticker will look perfect on one of my
Glitter Glam headbands.

I feel awesome and want to keep trying new things!

On the playground Gladys hears me singing to myself on the monkey bars.

She says my voice is unique! I didn't see it that way before.

I feel like playing possum, but I take a deep breath and say "Thank you," instead.

Maybe one day I'll sing in her group.

In the library I have to read at a poetry slam.
I really wish I could play possum.

But I remember how trying new things
has been okay once I decided to do them.

I finally get to the end of my poem, and everyone claps.

I'm proud of myself.

At lunch I want to talk to some girls wearing glittery shirts.

But what if they don't like me? I try to see it another way.

They must like glitter, and I do too; people are usually happy to talk about things they like!

So I say, "I like your sparkly style!"

Now they want to make Glitter Glam
headbands with me after school. I can't wait!

I still play possum when asked to do stuff like give a book report in front of the class,

try out for sports
I'm not very good at,

or act in a play.

But for now…

Ask me my name?

I'll tell you.

Invite me to play?

I'll think about it.

Want to be my friend?

I want to be yours, too.

I'm Blossom the Possum.
It's nice to meet you.

Note to Parents and Other Caregivers

by Julia Martin Burch, PhD

Blossom is a creative, playful, and artistic young possum. She is also very shy. There's nothing wrong with being shy; as many as 50% of kids describe themselves as "shy," and shy kids are often described by teachers as being more cooperative and better listeners. However, it's important for children to find a balance between feeling comfortable and challenging themselves to face their shyness so that they can do the things they value and enjoy.

Unchecked, shyness and anxiety can lead to a vicious cycle; when kids feel nervous and uncomfortable in a situation, they naturally try to avoid that activity or "freeze" up with fear, like Blossom does. But kids who miss out on these events also miss out on the opportunity to build important social skills, as well as the chance to learn that their fears did not come to pass. As kids continue to avoid or "freeze" and miss out on opportunities, these situations become even more intimidating and overwhelming, leading kids to continue to avoid them!

The good news is that parents and caretakers can do a lot to help support their shy child. Specifically...

Empathize and Validate

Create a safe and nonjudgmental space for your child to talk about what scares him. It is tempting for many parents—particularly naturally outgoing parents—to feel impatient with or frustrated by their hesitant, shy child. Do your best to be patient and to empathize with your child and validate the normalcy of their feelings. Share stories of times you have felt shy or anxious and of how you dealt with it.

Model and Practice

Children learn by watching you, so model the behaviors you want your child to develop. This includes appropriate social skills such as eye contact, smiles, a friendly greeting, and back and forth conversations and questions. Talk to your child about what she saw you do and help her practice those same skills with you. You might take turns "interviewing" each other to practice conversation, eye contact, and appropriate facial expressions. You can also help your child practice coping with nervous feelings. Though we cannot make tummy butterflies completely go away, doing things like taking deep, slow breaths from the belly or trying out some thinking strategies (described later in "Be a Detective!") can help. Additionally, consider modeling a willingness to approach fears of your own. For example, if you are afraid of heights, you might go on a Ferris Wheel with your child.

Be a Courage Coach

Most parents' natural inclination is to protect their child from uncomfortable and upsetting situations. However, as Blossom learns in the book, facing your fears can lead to fun experiences. It can also have a cumulative effect, leading to increased confidence in a variety of situations. Blossom's bravery in art class empowered her to play in band, speak up in class, and sing out! Continued practice helps kids realize that they can handle the feared situation and that the fun to come is worth the moment of anxiety. Allow your child to have these opportunities by stepping back and letting them try new things and face their fears. You can also set up opportunities for your child to feel good and successful when facing her fears, such as having a playdate centered around an activity she enjoys.

Your challenge as a parent is to cope with the uncertainty and anxiety of watching your child try something new and scary without immediately jumping in to help. Remember that coaches are always cheering from the sidelines and are there to help "after the game," to process both successes and failures. Challenge yourself to be like Mr. Brass, who validates Blossom's nervousness about playing a solo while simultaneously encouraging her to take a chance and see what happens.

Start Low, Go Slow

You can also help your child slowly and incrementally face the situations that make him nervous. For example, if your child would like to participate in the school play, but feels too nervous to audition, you could do fun practice auditions at home first with just you, then siblings, then possibly grandparents or neighbors. You could even see if your child could practice on the school stage before the real auditions. As your child becomes increasingly comfortable with performing in front of others, he learns that he is able to handle the anxiety that comes along with that performance. Additionally, the more time your child spends doing the things that scare him, the more he is able to "habituate," or have his anxiety decrease. Plus, the more your child practices in a variety of settings, the more those experiences will "generalize," or apply widely to different worries.

Your child can also practice things he might say to himself to keep his courage up in situations where he feels shy, such as "I have done this before and I can do it again now!" or "that's just shyness trying to push me around—I don't have to listen to it! I'm going to play my flute solo anyways!"

After your child faces a fear, you can help her process how it went, problem solve around any issues, and make a plan for next time. For example, you could say "I am so proud of your brave behavior at soccer tryouts! Was it scary as you thought it would be? Was there anything you would have liked to do differently?"

Be a Detective!

When Mr. Brass encourages Blossom to think of the situation in a different way, he is demonstrating flexible thinking. Helping your child think flexibly about anxiety-provoking situations is an important skill. Anxiety filters information from the environment through a lens that makes it seem threatening—and what we think affects how we feel! To help your child think more flexibly and "talk back" to their anxious thoughts, you can help your child "be a detective" and examine all of the different ways to look at a situation. For example, if your child fears that her classmates will all laugh at her during her presentation you might say, "That sounds like a really upsetting thought—I can understand why you feel nervous about tomorrow! I wonder if there are any other ways to look at the situation? If you were a detective looking for clues, you might think—how many times has the whole class laughed at me when I gave a speech? Have I ever seen that happen? I wouldn't like it if that happened, but could I survive?" Point out how when Blossom tried to "see it another way," she realized that even though Ramona played a few notes wrong, Blossom had still liked listening to her. This flexibility and detective thinking gives Blossom the mental wiggle room to take a chance and play herself.

As Blossom reflects in the book, "trying new things has been okay once I decided to do them." This is true for most kids as anticipatory anxiety, or the worry thoughts and feelings experienced while thinking about trying something new, is often far worse than the anxiety felt when actually facing that fear. Help your child reflect on times she had a lot of anticipatory anxiety and how things actually turned out, like a past party she was nervous about that ended up being fun.

Praise Effort and Bravery

Celebrate all of your child's attempts to face their fears! Focus on the effort, not the outcome. For example, if your child wanted to join a new group of kids on the playground, but ended up hanging back, you might say "I really love how you smiled in a friendly way at those kids. It can be hard to join in, but I know you would like to play with them. Would you like to talk about something you might say or do next time?" Come up with small, fun rewards your child can earn for facing his fears. Your child could get five minutes of sibling-free special time with you or could choose what the family has for dinner one night. As Blossom shows, even something small like a glitter sticker can be a highly motivating extra push to take a chance and be brave. Over time, rewards should be increasingly less necessary, as most kids quickly learn that the natural rewards for facing their fears, such as having fun with their friends, make a little anxiety worth it.

Shyness is normal, and chances are that there are some things that will always make your child feel nervous—just like Blossom continues to feel anxious when she has to give a book report or act in the play. However, by continuing to face their fears, children learn that no matter how uncomfortable or nervous they feel in the moment, that feeling eventually recedes (no one feels anxious forever!).

Seek Support

If your child's shyness or avoidance begins to cause them significant distress or impacts their functioning, you should consult with a licensed psychologist or other mental health professional who specializes in cognitive behavioral therapy (CBT) for children.

JULIA MARTIN BURCH, PhD, is a postdoctoral fellow in child and adolescent psychology at McLean Hospital. Dr. Martin Burch completed her training at Fairleigh Dickinson University and Massachusetts General Hospital/Harvard Medical School. She works with children, teens, and parents, and specializes in cognitive behavioral therapy for anxiety, obsessive compulsive, and related disorders.

About the Author

BIRDY JONES loves to tell stories. While living in Chicago, she taught underserved youth so they could find ways to tell their own stories, too. Her debut book *MISTER COOL* was named an Anti-Bullying Book of 2014 by *Publisher's Weekly*. She loves to write fiction and non-fiction picture books that inspires children to follow their dreams while being their own awesome selves! She currently lives with her husband and son in Wilmington, NC.

About the Illustrator

JANET MCDONNELL is an illustrator and author living in the calm outskirts of the windy city with her husband, two sons, and their black and white dog, Buster. Her whimsical illustrations combine traditional media and digital magic. In addition to illustrating books, magazines, and puzzles, Janet has both taught and written for children from preschool to high school ages.

About Magination Press

MAGINATION PRESS is an imprint of the American Psychological Association, the largest scientific and professional organization representing psychologists in the United States and the largest association of psychologists worldwide.